# KAMENGET...

## A REFLECTION OF MADRAS DIARIES

TEENA NANI

ISBN 979-888569064-5

# Contents

# Preface

I have a faint memory of how my father used to carry me around, as a toddler, and tell me these nice long stories to make me drink a cup of porridge. He would say the same sentence with so many different expressions and I would listen to him with rapt attention, with my mouth wide open. For every sentence he said, there would be a question from his side and an enthusiastic response from my side. To this day, the fascination and admiration for his story-telling continue. I still nag him to tell me stories of his childhood.

Now when I have children of my own, I try to replicate the same with them, in my own style though. My elder son nags me to tell him stories of my childhood. That's how I got interested in writing stories.

I was born and grew up in Madras, which is now called Chennai. Have lived most of my life there. So, the stories are based in the city of Madras and that is why the sub-title 'A reflection of Madras Diaries'.

Nitin, my elder son who is 10 yrs old now, has a way with drawing and sketching. I have seen him playing around with colors right from when he was 3 years old. He has a knack for creating drawings and I wanted to tap his talent, in fact, take advantage of it, for my book. Every single illustration in the book is a contribution from Nitin.

Hope you will enjoy them.

Acknowledgements

I would like to thank my life partner, my backbone, Sudhindra Sathyanarayana, for the encouragement and support that he has been giving me. In fact, he is the one who pushed me into publishing a book. He meticulously edits all my stories and gives me ideas on how to improve them.

A big thanks to my 10 year old son Nitinprivi Krsna Sudhindra, who is the illustrator for this book. He has worked hard on all the illustrations and given his best for it. Thanks to his art teacher, Mr. Pavan Kikkeri, for guiding him through all his sketches.

To my 5 year 'young' little one, for his big smile, umpteen thumbsups, and secret kisses, every time I achieved something. To my Parents-in-law for their tremendous support, encouragement and love.

Thanks to my Father, who has been my inspiration, and to my Mother for her unconditional love. And to all my Well-wishers who have given me tremendous support throughout this journey of mine.

# ONE

# THE NAME GAME TO FAME

"What is in a name?", you ask.
Yeah, that's right. What is in a name?

But it certainly can get very interesting, when it is your own name and when it is dissected, reshaped, misspelled and completely butchered into pieces without any sympathy, or even renovated into a totally new one without even the slightest of consideration. That's what happened to my name and continues to happen till date.

Your name is your identity. So, where shall I begin?

Okay, here goes.

Going back to the days when I was born, and when my parents were still deciding what to name me, my dad suddenly got this **lightning** of an idea, and decided to name me after the star sign I was born, along with my Grandma's name.

So, it shaped into "Thi" from Tiruvadirai, the name of the star and "Na" from Nakshatra, meaning star in our vernacular. Thankfully this combination culminated into being spelled "Teena" and not "Thina". As for my second name, "Nani", was derived from my grandmother's name "Naniamma", meaning someone who is shy. May be my dad just 'hoped against hope hopen' that I would be a shy girl. Sadly, I am anything, **but** that!

So begins the journey!

In my early childhood, the name Nani attracted a lot of teasing and bullying from my fellow mates. Here comes the dissecting part. "Nani", as is, in Hindi means Grandma and that meaning started getting associated to my name. So, I ensured all my texts and notebooks carried only my first name Teena.

I clearly tried avoiding the usage of the 'Nani' part of my name. At one point of time, I even tried to coax my parents into dropping my middle name from my government birth proof. The response was a stern nod of the head, sideways, from my father.

"I understand your predicament, child, but it's too much of a trouble going to modify the government issued document. Also, I want you to consider your father's sentiments. Don't you worry, you shall get used to your name.", was the consoling words from my sympathetic mother.

Yes, as she said, I started getting used to the myriads of ways in which my name got utilized. Here comes the misspelling part. People called me Teena Rani, Teena Mani, Teena Mari, Teena Naari*, Teena Nari** and myriad other names.

*Naari - Stinky in Tamil
**Nari- Fox in Tamil

The best part was when a Postman came to our address and called out from the doorsteps, "Thinamani! Thinamani!". Coincidentally, I came out to answer him and told that we had not subscribed to the newspaper named "Thinamani". The Postman gave me a stern look, cleared his throat, and told me in a rather strict tone that it was *for* Thinamani and asserted that he was not mistaken about the address he had arrived at.

As surprised as I was with his reply, and also baffled, I took a peek at the post card that he was holding for Thinamani, and checked the address. It then all fell in place and made me realize... the butchering part. The postman had just completely slaughtered my **Beautiful** name in a way that no one else could!

My family members had a good laugh at my expense and I continued to disapprove such a silly thing happened with my name. But, hey, as it is said in the Bhagavad Gita, "Everything happens for a reason!".

There was this once, when I had been to a National Level Japanese Speech Contest in Delhi. The contest went well, and me, along with the other participants, were anxiously waiting for the results.

I was awestruck at how fluently Mr. Ashok Chawla, a very renowned Japanese language expert, who was also the host for the evening, spoke in Japanese.

When it was time for the results, he called out a name, and did so without even looking at the list. "...and the third place goes to... Ms. Nani".

That took me by surprise, I was still sitting dumb in my seat, not realizing that it was my name which was being announced. My father, who was beside, nudged me, and then it all came flooding to me. I had just won the prize and was being addressed by that part of my name which had been causing all the above comical moments. I was to go and get the prize.

**That**! was the moment I realized how very different "Nani" in my name actually is, and how much of a recognition it could bring me. The person on stage, didn't even give the list a second glance, he remembered my name for its uniqueness!

Now, stands the day when I don't crib about it. On the contrary, I introduce myself with my full name. In fact, later in my life, time for reckoning, when I got the opportunity to go to Japan and represent India, there I introduced myself as 'Teena Nani'. Some of my colleagues were amused.

The reason being that 'Nani' means 'What' in Japanese. So, I said on a lighter note to them -

"I know you are still comprehending the name 'Teena **Nani**'???"

"...are you thinking Teena-What?"

"I am 'Teena Nani' and that is what I will always be."

Now, when I get called, 'Teena Navi' or

'Teena Nali' or even

'Thinamani', I don't react to it.

I step forward, and only respond with a smile and gently correct them-

"You'll not forget it! The names Nani - ***TEENA NANI***".

# TWO

# KAMENGET KAMARKAT

"Meenu, Meenu", mom called out to me. I was busy making a chain for my toy.

"Would you please come quick child!", she yelled from the kitchen.

"Coming, mom!", I ran to find out what the emergency was.

"Meenu, can you quickly run to the corner shop and get me some ginger? I need it for the curry. It's almost lunch time and your dad will come home any minute now." She went rattling at the speed of a bullet train.

"The Corner Shop??", I was still stuck in the first sentence.

"Yes, the one in North Mada street." But that was 4 streets away. Yeah, technically it was in a corner but not in the corner of our street.

Well, I had no choice. Mom just thrust 2 rupees into my hand and literally pushed me out. Actually, I didn't mind going out. I was anyways getting bored playing by myself.

As I stepped out of my house and started walking towards the shop, I could faintly hear a bell ring and a vendor scream out

"Kamarkat....Kamarkat...Kam-n-get....Kamarkat...".

A few boys ran to the next street. I walked a little faster to see what was so interesting with the "**Kamenget*... Kamarkat****".

The vendor was already surrounded by young boys handing over money and buying the delicacy.

The way they popped it into their mouths and moved it around in a circular motion, made it extremely tempting.

Their "oohs" and "aahs" and the wide grin on their faces only added to my temptation and curiosity.

Just looking at them was enough to send my taste buds on a marathon. My mouth was watering and I badly wanted to taste the "Kamenget...Kamarkat".

The vendor's voice and the potential taste of the candy, pulled me like a magnet.

Unable to resist the temptation, I looked into my hands to assess my financial situation. Mom had given me 2 rupees. Even if I spent 20 paise to buy myself 2 of those "Kamenget...Kamarkats", I would still have 1 rupee 60 paise remaining...I frowned...No no no no...wait wait...I would have 1 rupee 80 paise remaining....good...I was getting better at math now.

So if I were to buy 1 rupee 80 paise worth of ginger, it still would be a big enough piece and mom would never know that I had borrowed a few paisas off her money...I smiled. Then I grinned. Great then! Time to relish some "Kamenget... Kamarkats".

I walked up to the vendor and bought myself 2 of them. They looked more like brown coloured candys. This was the first time I was tasting them and they were real yummy...I rolled them around in my mouth, enjoying the sweet nectar that flowed down my throat. Now that my wish was fulfilled, I moved towards my actual goal.

I reached the vegetable shop. Pushing one "Kamenget...kamarkat" to each side of my cheek, I asked for ginger. The shopkeeper peered at me with eyebrows raised. I must have looked like a Puffer fish to him, with my cheek puffed up on both sides. "Are you alright child? Hope you are not coming down with some illness...". "I am fine, uncle. Thank you", moving my mouth like a fish breathing in water. He grunted, "Ginger? For how much?". I stretched out my hand to show him the change I had. He took it from me, wrapped up some ginger in a piece of newspaper and handed it over to me.

Mission accomplished. Now, I walk back home to hand it over to mom. On my way back, I stood a while to watch some boys play cricket in the playground.

I was still gaping at the game, when I was jolted out of my reverie. "Meenu, Meenu.." I heard my mom calling out to me. I started running to reach the finish line when I realized that I still had the "**Kamenget...Kamarkats**" in my mouth. I bit into those candies to quickly finish them but hey! What's this! They stuck to my teeth and I couldn't seem to chew them. I tried again to chew them but they were so sticky, I just couldn't open my mouth.

Mom was waiting in front of the gate, with an irritated

look on her face. She grabbed the ginger from my hands, and rushed inside to finish her curry. Meanwhile I was still struggling to chew these sticky, yet delicious bits of "Kamenget...Kamarkats".

Once she finished preparing the curry, Mom called out to me again. But this time to enquire about something.

"Meenu, why did the shopkeeper give you a lesser quantity of ginger today?".

I looked at her with surprise. How did she find out? I gave her a casual shrug as if to say, "How would I know?" and turned to go, when mom caught my hand.

She turned me around and asked in a calm but stern voice, "Meenu, did he say the prices have gone up?".

I shook my head.

She looked at me curiously and asked, "Did you buy something else?".

I turned red.

"Why are you not answering me?".

I opened my mouth to answer but the sticky candy wouldn't let my teeth apart.

"Did he cheat you?"

I opened my mouth to say "I really don't know", but somehow, it felt like I had drunk a cup full of some super glue which had my teeth stuck fast together.

Looking at how fidgety and nervous I was, explaining only with gestures, and not opening my mouth, mom stretched a stiff hand to hold my face by the chin, and asked me to open my mouth.

My eyes brimmed and one little drop of tear flowed out.

Mom became concerned and immediately dropped her stern look. Instead, now she held my chin with a loving hand and made me look up into her eyes. She seemed to understand what was happening.

"Hmm...Run now to the washroom and spit out whatever you are chewing on."

I rushed to the washroom to embrace my best friend for that moment, the Toothbrush!

After brushing for more than a quarter hour, I managed to get out the last piece of the godforsaken, yet delicious "**Kamenget...**Kamarkat".

Mom was waiting, ready to fire a thousand questions and may be a long lecture.

"So Meenu, now tell me what kept you so long and what is it that you were eating."

"I was watching a cricket match", I sulked, conveniently ignoring the second question.

"Ok. And what was it that you were munching on?"

"Kamenget...Kamarkat", I answered in a feeble note.

"Kamenget...what?"

"Kamenget...Kamarkat"

"I have never heard of anything like "Kamengetkamarkat" before", she frowned.

"But it was very tasty mom. It is this round, brown candy that stays in your mouth for a looooong time."

"What did you say the candy was?"

"**Kamenget...**Kamarkat"

Mom frowned again and then it came to her. It was a revelation!

She laughed. She laughed and laughed and laughed and finally grabbed me, gave me a hug, holding me with delight for my childish innocence. She wrapped her left hand around my waist and said "Oh sweety, thats a Kamarkattu that you had. An age old sweet that we have been having from our childhood and that which even our ancestors relished."

"Next time you want to eat something, ask me. Don't go ahead and buy it yourself. You don't want to end up with a bad tummy, do you?"

I nodded a no.

"So it's a Kamarkattu that had kept your mouth tight shut, because of its stickiness due to the jaggery and coconut paste-mix. Next time, I want some peace in the house, I shall pop a Kamarkattu in your mouth.", she said with a big smile. "I shall ask your dad to buy a packet full of

Kamarkattus for you."

I was happy. Not just for the future "**Kamenget...**Kamarkat" I would get, but also that I escaped a nice good spanking.

Now, that's a sweet ending to my story.

Care to taste a "**Kamenget...**Kamarkattu"?

Then, come over and we can have a feast! :-)

* **Kamenget** - The vendor's version of 'Come and get'

** **Kamarkattu** or **Kamarkat** is an age old snack made at home, and is basically a candy made with jaggery and coconut

# THREE

# A RAT-TLING DISCOVERY

"I am going to kill that rat for wreaking my kitchen! How dare it raid my kitchen like this!", I screamed, outraged at the way the rat had eaten up all my food items and soiled the containers. I was distraught at the thought of cleaning up the entire kitchen for the third time that month.

Enough of this house! I wanted to vacate the place that very moment. But my husband calmly asked me to relax and not to worry, since he promised to help clean the kitchen. True to his words, he helped me clean up the place and I was back to my normal self. We had tactfully closed the hole through which that pesky rat was sneaking in. Nevertheless, I had kept a thick stick next to my bed and was prepared to beat the daylights out of that rat, if I happened to spot it again.

One week later, when I was blissfully sleeping in my bed upstairs, I dreamt of that dreadful rat again. The same scratching sound, the same toppling of vessels. I woke up with a start.

'This hyperactive imagination of mine won't even let me sleep', I mumbled and went back to sleep.

'Clang' Ah! That same sound resonated through the house!

Oh No! Not again!

I tried waking my husband. But he continued his slumber, not budging a wee bit.

I decided to deal with this myself and grabbed the stick and stealthily tiptoed down the stairs to catch the culprit, red-handed. I somehow felt like a ninja in those Japanese movies!!

But when I peeped in to the kitchen, what I saw sent a shiver down my spine. It wasn't a rat this time!! I saw the figure of a man searching for something to eat. He found the idlis, which are steamed rice cakes popular in South India, that I had so lovingly made for my husband for his breakfast and started gorging it up.

I ran upstairs with wobbly knees to wake my husband up.

I frantically woke him, half whispering and half screeching that there was an intruder in the house. My husband sleepily appealed to me to go back to sleep, saying we will take care of the issue in the morning.

"You don't understand!" I lamented.

"Nobody understands you like I do, darling. Just go back to sleep. We will deal with it in daylight".

"Oh, you don't understand! There is a thief in our house! And he is stealing my IDLIS!", I almost yelled.

"Oh!", he sat up on the bed, rubbed his eyes and told me in a saint-like tone, "Then relax! You needn't worry at all. He doesn't know he has walked into a trap!"
No sooner did he finish saying it, we heard a heavy thud.

We rushed to the kitchen. Actually I was the one who rushed, my husband was ambling behind me.
I was surprised to see the thief sprawled on the kitchen floor. He was out cold, choking on my 'idlis'!

I turned to look at my husband with a confused look and he said, "Didn't I tell you? Nobody understands you and your skills like I do", with a wide grin.

# FOUR
# THE HOLY BOX

On this hot summer day, the kids returned from school as usual, ravenously hungry. After attending to them and ensuring their tummies were full, the ladies in our family, as is our usual ritual, sat down in front of the holy box to watch the nation-wide time pass of the millennia, the most interesting and all-consuming mega serials.

We ladies, the 5 'Star' sisters, had been watching this particular TV series, for the last 4 or more years and only the almighty knew when it would cease to exist. Surely, even the story writer himself had no idea where or how to end it. Whereas, the grumpy men of the house smirked at such waste of time. But the women considered it a daily ritual, which no one could afford to miss.

Even while someone had to go out on an errand, we ensured we were back by the time the serial would start. If circumstances demanded that we miss it, then there was always the counterpart sister to call up to get updates on the missed episodes, that too with the due diligence of frame-by-frame narration.

Yes, on this day, it was that time of the evening when we were all hurriedly finishing up all our chores and settling down in front of the TV. One of us who had already settled down, was ready and held the remote like a holy grail in her hands.

She pressed the 'ON' button on the remote.

The TV wouldn't switch-on.

Something was not alright.

She immediately called out to me, 'Rinku, Rinku'. I came in to find out what the matter was. Then, I took the remote and started pressing on the most logically right buttons.

When that didn't work, I took a chance and most anxiously and rigorously pressed the 'number' buttons on the remote.

Anxiety of losing the episode was writ across my sister's face.

Still, the TV would not switch on.

Then, my sister grabbed the remote from me and did what we had learnt from our elders, the next logical thing.

Guess what? Banging the remote on the palm of her hand. As if spanking the life out of it would help.

Only, you wouldn't hear the remote scream out loud, for it was begging to leave it alone, in the other parallel universe, where it could talk.

Still, nothing happened! The TV continued to remain blank.

Now, in comes our sister-in-law.

"Sonam. There seems to be something wrong with the remote. Can you check?", my sister pleaded.

Of the 5 of us, Sonam was the most technical. Looking at sweat bubbles popping on our foreheads, she decided to verify the next logical step.

It was now time for the remote to undergo reincarnation, that is, to die and to come alive. Sonam was going to operate, I mean, cut open the remote. She placed the remote down on its surgical bed, the coffee table in the hall.

She turned the remote face down and opened the slot to the batteries. The remote was suffocating, like a pinned down swine, trying hard to escape his shackles with his face pressed down to the coffee table. It smelt of dried up tea drops, left over biscuit bits and a dusty newspaper. In his universe, the remote was screaming and begging for mercy, dreading his impending fate.

Sonam checked to see if the batteries were loose or out-of-charge. She quickly grabbed a set of new batteries that her son had bought for his remote controlled car and swapped it with the older ones.

Now, the remote felt relieved and happy that he was replenished with a fresh lease of energy from the new set of batteries. In his universe, the remote was smiling and staring at his brother, the TV.

Sonam pressed the buttons of the remote once again hoping for a positive sign.

Negative. The TV remained unresponsive.

By now the entire battalion of ladies had assembled on the war front. Each one sweating out buckets, staring at the blank screen of the TV. Each one trying to figure out what could have gone wrong?

Was it a problem with the cable connection?

No.

In that case, the TV would switch-on and at least show the standard DD1 channels.

The TV, in his universe, had simply fallen asleep with his eyes closed shut.

"Maybe the picture tube is gone", someone suggested.

Everyone looked at her in dismay. Was it Doomsday!

"No, No. It can't be that. It must be some transmission fault.", we wished.

By now, all of us were a bundle of nerves. Some clinging to their "lucky charm" necklace lockets, some standing with folded hands, eyes looking towards the sky, and yet some, sending out a silent prayer, hoping for a miracle to happen.

"Call Pintu or Monu. They will fix the problem. Whatever it is.", called out one, jolting us all out of our reverie.

"Oh, but they are gone for their tuition and their teacher doesn't appreciate any disturbances in between.", replied the proud, yet, troubled mother, my second eldest sister, Kirti.

"Oh, No!", "It is indeed Dooms day, cometh", our eldest sister, Kajal groaned.

Then, the youngest sister-in-law, Swathi, started frantically searching for the contact number of the TV mechanic. “Let’s see if we can get him to come before the serial ends.”

“Please bhaiyya, come fast. It is urgent.” she had requested a known TV mechanic, to come visit and take a look at the beloved TV.

Meanwhile, we all sat sullen faced.

"I wonder if he will leave her at this stage.”

“I don’t think he should. She is terminally ill. How can he leave her at this stage!”

“But, he has no idea that she is not well na. The stupid female won’t even reveal it to him. She wants to bottle it all up inside herself until the end.”

The clouds got darker in our heads. We became gloomier after the discussion.

The passion and involvement with which the discussion went on, one would think we were discussing about our own sibling. Little would anybody know that the discussion was about the characters in the serial.

Suddenly Sonam burst out “I wonder what is taking him so long?”

“To realize that she is not well you mean?”

“Noooo! The mechanic! He is taking ages to reach here." She turned to Swathi, "Can you call him again?”.

Swathi was just about to call him, when the mechanic stepped in.

He was immediately confronted by the battalion of sisters, lined up and ready to bombard him.

“What took you so long???”

The TV mechanic, simply ignored the comment and went ahead to find out what was wrong. He picked up the remote and tried switching on the TV. When it didn’t come alive, he went to peek behind the TV.

“Is there something wrong with the picture tube?”, someone asked with bated breath, still clutching her lucky charm.

The mechanic silently spent a few seconds behind the TV, then the sleeping ‘Kumbhakarna’ came alive.

“Wow! Tussi great ho bhaiyya.”, I said with glee, meaning ‘You are great, brother’.

The rain and shower of praises started pouring in.

“How much for the repairs?”, my eldest sister asked.

The TV mechanic was swift in his demand, “100 rupees Ma’am”, he said.

"Only so much? How sweet. We would have given you a 1000, had you asked for it." blurted my delighted sister.

"What was wrong?"

The mechanic waited till he got the money into his hands. He smiled and said "The TV was unplugged and it was not connected."

It was now the ladies' turn to look at each other and give a totally blank look.

The smart mechanic left the house with a sardonic smile.

9 798885 690645

Printed by Libri Plureos GmbH in Hamburg, Germany